MR. M
go to the zoo
Roger Hargreaves

WITHDRAWN

Hello, my name is Walter. Can you spot me in this book?

Original concept by
Roger Hargreaves

Written and illustrated by
Adam Hargreaves

B000 000 020 9863

ABERDEEN LIBRARIES

It was Sunday.

And Little Miss Naughty had lots of jobs to do around the house.

Her bed needed making.

The house needed cleaning.

And the garden needed weeding.

So what did Little Miss Naughty do?

She went to the zoo!

Bed making was not fun.

Cleaning was not fun.

And weeding was not fun.

But the zoo?

The zoo was fun.

The first place that Little Miss Naughty visited at the zoo was the monkey house.

Little Miss Naughty liked the monkeys, they were just as naughty as she was.

And as we all know she does enjoy being naughty.

But there was someone else at the zoo who also liked being naughty.

Mr Mischief!

Mr Mischief watched Little Miss Naughty feed
Mr Greedy's iced buns to the elephant.

Which was very naughty.

And this got Mr Mischief thinking.

Not to be outdone, Mr Mischief let the lion out of his cage at feeding time!

Luckily, Mr Strong was on hand to put things right.

Little Miss Naughty was rather put out.

She wanted to be the naughtiest.

She had to be the naughtiest.

So she fed Little Miss Splendid's hat to the hippo!

But, as quick as a flash, Mr Mischief had painted stripes on the leopard …

… and spots on the zebra.

Poor Mr Muddle was in even more of a muddle than usual.

Little Miss Naughty had to think hard.

She could not let Mr Mischief beat her.

She crept into the reptile house and gave Little Miss Shy a terrible shock with the hose.

Hissss!

Things were getting out of hand.

Mr Mischief climbed up the giraffe's neck and dropped an ice cream on the top of Mr Tall's head.

Little Miss Naughty poured food colouring in the penguin pool and turned it pink.

The zoo was in chaos.

And the zookeeper was very unhappy.

Very unhappy indeed!

And then, Mr Mischief and Little Miss Naughty decided to have an ostrich race.

The winner would be declared the naughtiest of all.

And it was the naughtiest one of them who won.

Mr Mischief.

He painted glue on the feet of Little Miss Naughty's ostrich.

And because Little Miss Naughty's ostrich was so slow, the zookeeper was able to catch her in his net.

As a punishment he set her to work.

He set her to work on a very big job.

Cleaning up behind the elephant!

Maybe Little Miss Naughty should have stayed
at home ...

... and cleaned up her own mess.

Suddenly, cleaning the house did not seem so bad after all!